Top Place Percy

Peter Bently

Illustrated by Daniel Howarth

NEW
BURLINGTON
BOOKS

Percy Plaice is going to the fair.

His friend Sprat *whizzes* past.
"See you at the fair, slowcoach!" calls Sprat.

"I wish I was as zippy as Sprat," thinks Percy.

Angelfish nearly **bumps** into Percy.

"Sorry, Percy!" she says. "It's hard to see you among all the mud and rocks and seaweed."

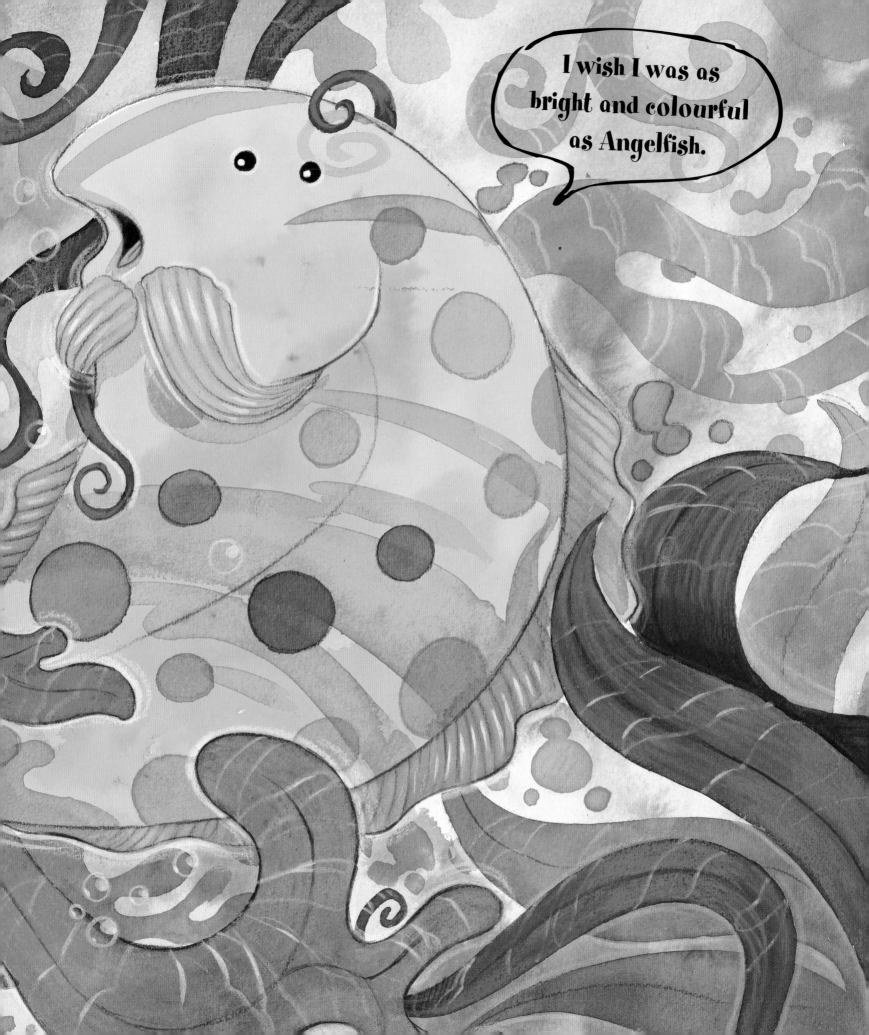

Pufferfish tumbles by and **puffs** himself up
like a big spiky balloon.
Everyone laughs.

"I wish I was a cool, fun shape
like Pufferfish," thinks Percy.

Percy and his friends have great fun at the *fair*.

They ride on the big wheel...

the merry-go-round...

the helter-skelter...

and the dodgems.

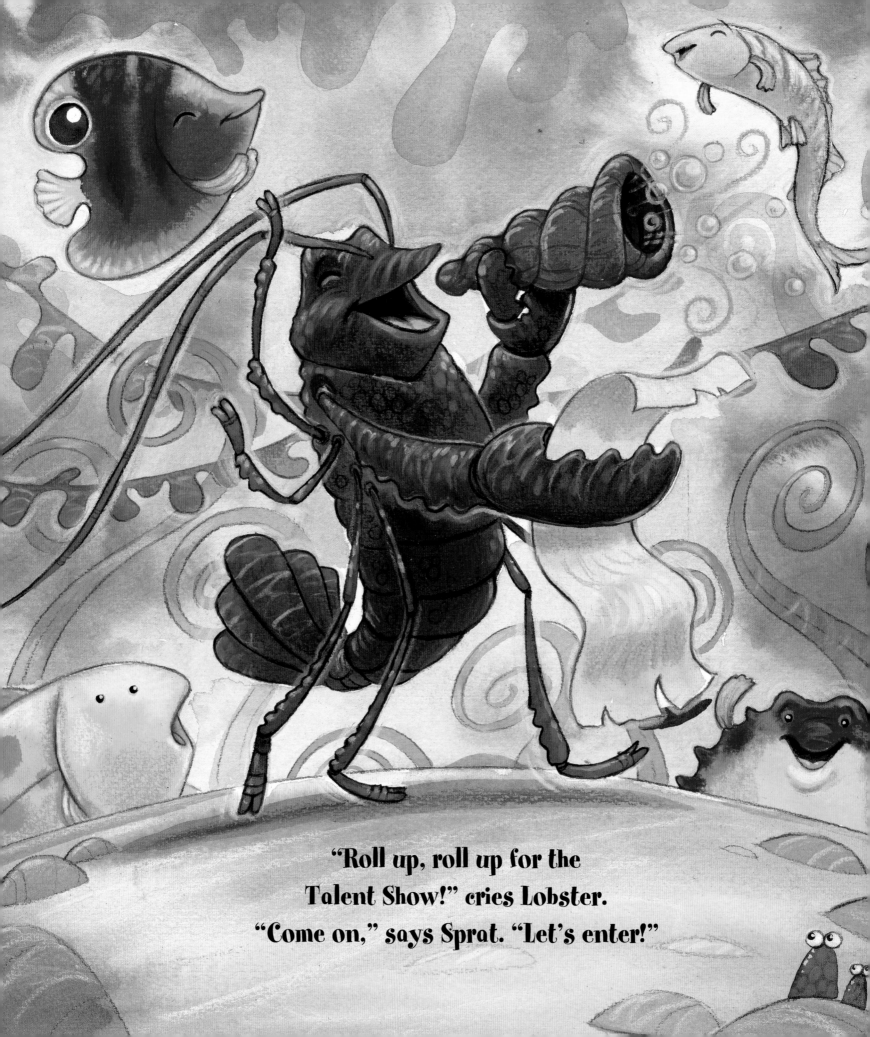

"Roll up, roll up for the
Talent Show!" cries Lobster.
"Come on," says Sprat. "Let's enter!"

Sprat enters
the competition
for the
FASTEST FISH,

Angelfish enters
the competition
for the MOST
COLOURFUL FISH,

and Pufferfish enters the competition for the FUNNIEST FISH.

"Aren't you going to enter the Talent Show, Percy?" asks Angelfish.

"There's no point," sighs Percy, swimming sadly away. "I'm nobody special. Only a slow, dull, flat, boring fish."

Suddenly, Percy's three friends *race* towards him.

HELP!

"HELP!" cries Sprat. "Shark is coming!
I might be fast but he's much faster than me!"

"If only I wasn't so colourful!" gasps Angelfish.
"**Shark** will spot me easily!"

"Me too!" wails Pufferfish. "I don't think he feels like laughing!"
"**Don't panic!**" says Percy. "I've got an idea."

"Tee-hee!" cackles **Shark**. "I just saw some tasty-looking fish nipping behind that rock. It's time for my dinner!"

He swims **closer**,

and closer,

and closer,

and finds...

"Bah!" grumbles Shark. "Only mud and rocks and seaweed!"

And with a flick of his tail he speeds off.

"Phew!" says Sprat.
"Thanks for hiding us, Percy. That was close!"

Nice one, Percy!

"Let's get back to the fair," says Sprat.
"Lobster is announcing the winners of the Talent Show!"

FASTEST FISH:
Sprat!
MOST COLOURFUL FISH:
Angelfish!
FUNNIEST FISH:
Pufferfish!
1st
1st
1st

"But **Top Place** in the Talent Show goes to...
PERCY PLAICE!"

"For being the Best at Hiding
and the Best at Helping your Friends," says Lobster.

"Hooray for Percy!" cheers Pufferfish.
"It's Top Place for a Top Plaice!"

Notes for parents and teachers

- Look at the cover together before reading the book. Can the children think what the story is about?

- Read the story and then ask the children to read it to you. Help them with any unfamiliar words and praise them for their efforts.

- Can the children remember all the different types of sea creatures in the story? Which ones are their favourites? Do they know where they live? Have they ever seen them in real life?

- Being different is an important topic in this story. Percy thinks he is not special enough to win a prize. But in the end he saves his friends from the shark and wins the best prize of all. Ask the children what makes Percy special (his camouflage, bravery and quick thinking or something else), and discuss how everyone is special in some way.

- Another key theme of the story is friendship. Discuss what the story tells children about being friends. What makes a good friend?

- Act out the story as a play. One child can be Percy and four others can play his friends Pufferfish, Angelfish and Sprat, and of course Shark. The other children can be all sorts of other fish and sea creatures. How do these fish and creatures move?

- Ask the children to draw and colour in lots of different types of fish. They can draw real creatures or colourful fantasy fish. Cut the fish out and make a big collage.

Editor: Alexandra Koken
Designer: Chris Fraser

Copyright © QED Publishing 2011

A NEW BURLINGTON BOOK
First published in the UK in 2011 by
QED Publishing
Part of The Quarto Group
The Old Brewery, 6 Blundell Street
London N7 9BH

www.qed-publishing.co.uk

A catalogue record for this book is available from the British Library.

ISBN 978 1 84835 756 3

Printed in China